Here's what kids and teachers have to say to Ron Roy, author of the A to Z Mysteries series:

"Josh is super cool!
He is almost as cool as me!"
—Zack M.-H.

"I like the way you put a lot of
adventure in your books."—Christie C.

"The A to Z Mysteries really get me thinking.
When I pick up an A to Z Mystery book,
it's hard to put down."—Erica F.

"Thank you for your books.
I am enjoying them as much as my students."
—JoAnn D.

P is for PUBLIC LIBRARY. The Panda Puzzle
*is dedicated to libraries and librarians, who help
kids find wonderful books to read. Thank you!*
—R.R.

To Ron, for writing a great series.
—J.S.G.

Text copyright © 2002 by Ron Roy
Illustrations copyright © 2002 by John Steven Gurney
All rights reserved under International and Pan-American Copyright
Conventions. Published in the United States by Random House, Inc.,
New York, and simultaneously in Canada by Random House of
Canada Limited, Toronto.

www.randomhouse.com/kids
www.ronroy.com

Library of Congress Cataloging-in-Publication Data
Roy, Ron.
The panda puzzle / by Ron Roy ; illustrated by John Steven Gurney.
p.   cm. — (A to Z mysteries)   "A stepping stone book."
Summary: Dink, Josh, and Ruth Rose investigate the kidnapping
of the new baby panda at the petting zoo.
ISBN 0-375-80271-1 (trade) — ISBN 0-375-90271-6 (lib. bdg.)
[1. Giant panda—Fiction. 2. Pandas—Fiction. 3. Zoos—Fiction.
4. Mystery and detective stories.] I. Gurney, John, ill. II. Title.
PZ7.R8139 Pan 2002   [Fic]—dc21   2001019541

Printed in the United States of America   First Edition   February 2002
10 9 8 7 6 5 4

A to Z Mysteries

The Panda Puzzle

by Ron Roy

illustrated by
John Steven Gurney

A STEPPING STONE BOOK™

Random House New York

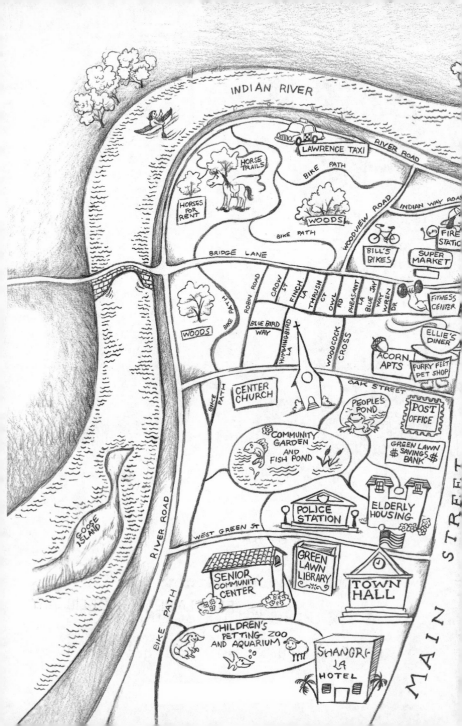

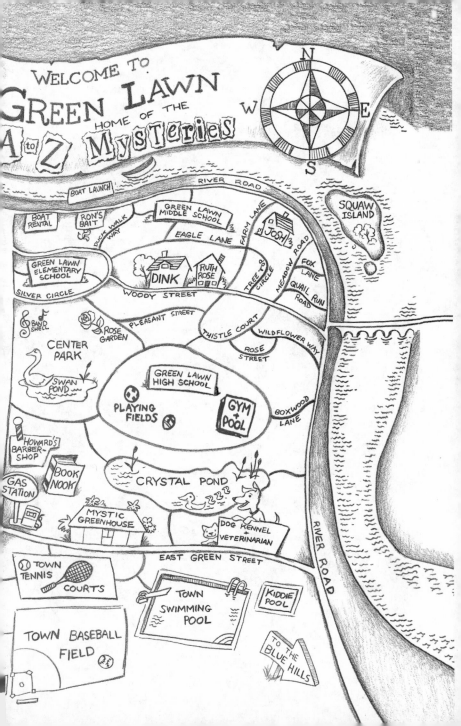

CHAPTER 1

"I can't believe Green Lawn has its own pandas," Ruth Rose said. She held up her dad's camcorder. "I hope I can get them on videotape!"

Ruth Rose always dressed in one color. Today, she wore sky blue from head to toe.

Ruth Rose, her little brother, Nate, and her friends Dink and Josh were visiting the petting zoo. A mother panda and her baby had arrived just the day before!

All four kids stood in the middle of

a crowd near the panda enclosure. Dink recognized a lot of his friends from school. He waved at Officer Fallon and his grandson, Jimmy.

Through the skinny rails of the enclosure fence, the kids could see a cave and a pool of water. Bamboo grew beside the cave.

From his pocket, Dink pulled out a folded paper. It was an issue of *The Panda Paper*. The front-page story was all about how the pandas, Ping and Winnie, had come to Green Lawn. The headline was PETTING ZOO PERFECT PLACE FOR PANDAS!

"I'm going to ask the editor if I can write a story about the baby panda," Dink said.

Josh was chomping on an apple and holding Pal's leash. "If you do, I'll draw its picture for you," he said.

"Can I play with the panda?" asked Nate.

"Sorry, Natie," Ruth Rose said. "Pandas only like to play with *other* pandas."

Nate was on tiptoes. "I can't see," he complained. "There's too many big people."

"There's a bench over there," Dink said. "We can see better if we stand on it."

The four kids climbed onto a nearby bench. Now they could see over the crowd. Pal flopped on the lawn with a big sigh and closed his eyes.

The crowd stood just outside the fence. Off to one side, standing near a microphone, were two men and a woman.

The kids recognized the woman. Her name was Irene Napper, and she worked at the petting zoo. She fed the animals and made sure they were safe and comfortable. She was wearing a green uniform with the words PETTING ZOO stitched onto her shirt pocket.

Next to Irene was a short man with spiky yellow hair. That was Tom Steele, the editor of *The Panda Paper*.

"Who's the guy wearing the necktie?" Josh asked.

The man Josh had asked about was very tan. He was whispering something to Irene Napper.

"That's Flip Frances," Dink said. He showed Josh a picture in *The Panda Paper*. "His grandmother gave the money to Green Lawn to build this park."

Just then, Flip Frances spoke into the microphone. "Can you all hear me?" he asked.

Ruth Rose turned on the camcorder and aimed it toward the microphone.

"Hi, everyone, I'm Flip Frances," he said. "As many of you know, it was my grandmother, Winifred Frances, who made Panda Park possible. Granny Win would be happy that you all came to meet little Winnie. And I'm pleased that her money went to such a good cause."

He turned to Irene Napper. "Irene is taking good care of our new arrivals," he said, handing her the microphone.

"Thanks, Flip," Irene said into the mike. "I just want to say that I've loved getting to know little Winnie. She's a happy, playful baby."

Irene passed the mike to Tom Steele. "Hello, everyone," the editor said. "As you know, *The Panda Paper* has a very small staff—me! I could use some help. I'd love to print your stories, poems, or pictures about pandas."

Tom Steele grinned. "But I can't pay you anything!"

Everyone in the crowd laughed.

Just then, a black-and-white face appeared inside the cave's entrance.

The crowd quieted. Slowly, the mother panda moved into the sunlight. Her head swiveled around and she lifted her nose into the air. Suddenly she charged the fence and threw her body against the metal rails.

Tom Steele, Irene Napper, and Flip Frances leaped back. People at the front of the crowd jumped back, too.

"What's wrong with her?" Ruth Rose asked, catching it all on videotape.

Ping stared through the bars of the fence. After a minute, she waddled back into her cave.

A man in a green uniform hurried over to Irene Napper. Irene handed him her keys, and the man unlocked the fence gate. Carefully, he crossed over to the cave, knelt down, and looked inside.

Then he reached in and pulled something out. To Dink, it looked like a round alarm clock. A small piece of paper was tied around it with a string. The man relocked the gate and handed the object to Irene. She removed the paper and silently read what was written on it.

"This is so weird!" Josh whispered. "What's going on?"

Irene stepped back to the microphone. Dink noticed her hand was shaking.

"This is a ransom note," Irene told the crowd. "Winnie has been kid-napped!"

THE PANDA PAPER

PETTING ZOO PERFECT PLACE FOR PANDAS!

CHAPTER 2

"KIDNAPPED!" Ruth Rose gasped.

Everyone in the crowd began talking at once. Officer Fallon ran to talk to Irene.

"Where's Winnie?' Nate asked. "I want to see Winnie!"

"Winnie has gone away for a little while," Ruth Rose told her little brother.

"Where?" the four-year-old insisted.

Ruth Rose put her arm around Nate's shoulders. "We don't know yet," she said.

Officer Fallon stepped up to the microphone. "Folks, you might as well go home," he said. "We have every reason to believe that Winnie is safe. We'll do our best to get her back."

Tom Steele, Flip Frances, and Irene Napper left Panda Park together.

Officer Fallon and Jimmy began walking around the outside of the panda enclosure.

The crowd slowly wandered away.

"What a lousy thing to do!" Josh said, helping Nate down from the bench.

"What's going to happen to Winnie?" Ruth Rose asked. "Doesn't she need her mother to feed her?"

Dink glanced at the story in *The Panda Paper*. "It says Winnie's almost six months old," he said. "She's eating by herself now."

"Come on," said Ruth Rose. "Let's go talk to Officer Fallon."

The kids caught up with the police chief and his grandson outside the fence behind the bamboo forest. Pal flopped on his belly and stuck his nose through the fence rails. Nate sat next to him and patted the dog's head.

"Hey, kids," Officer Fallon said. "Some situation, eh?"

"The kidnappers want a million bucks for Winnie!" Jimmy Fallon blurted out.

"Jimmy!" his grandfather said.

"Is it true?" Ruth Rose asked.

Officer Fallon nodded. "I'm afraid that's what this says," he said. Holding the note by its edges, he let the kids inspect it.

Josh read the note aloud:

"Leave one million dollars in the hollow tree on Goose Island by midnight tonight. No tricks, or you'll never see Winnie again."

"A MILLION DOLLARS!" Ruth

Rose cried. "Where would Green Lawn get all that money?"

"As I recall," Officer Fallon said, "there's still over a million left from the money Winifred Frances left. The kidnapper must know that."

Dink examined the note. "What does the kidnapper mean by 'tricks'?" he asked.

"He means we shouldn't put any police officers on the island to catch him when he comes for the money," Officer Fallon said. "Or tamper with the bills so we can trace them."

Ruth Rose studied the ransom note. "These letters were cut out of a newspaper," she said.

"Yes," Officer Fallon said. "Which means we can't trace the note."

Suddenly Pal let out a woof. He stuck a paw through the fence and began scratching.

Josh bent down to see what Pal was doing. "Guys, look!" he said.

Partly hidden among the bamboo stalks was something shiny.

"It's a knife!" Jimmy Fallon said.

Officer Fallon got down on his knees. "It sure is," he said. He scratched Pal behind the ears. "Good dog!"

Officer Fallon stuck a long arm through the fence and picked up the knife. He brought it out, being careful not to cut himself.

The knife had a thin blade and a fat handle made of cork.

"Looks like a fishing knife," Officer Fallon said. "If the knife gets dropped in the water, the handle will float."

"Can I have it, Grandpa?" Jimmy asked.

"Afraid not, Jimmy," Officer Fallon said. "This is evidence." He drew a clean handkerchief from his pocket and carefully wrapped the knife.

"Hey, look at this," Josh said. He reached through the fence and pulled back a stalk of bamboo. The top had been sliced neatly off.

"There's more," Josh said, pointing through the fence. "Someone cut a bunch of this stuff."

"Maybe the kidnapper took some bamboo to feed Winnie," Ruth Rose said.

"At least she won't be hungry," Josh said.

"That explains the knife," Officer Fallon said. "With a struggling panda in his arms, the kidnapper probably never knew he dropped it."

Officer Fallon reached into his pocket. He pulled out the object that had been found in Ping's cave. "Know what this is?" he asked.

"It looks like an alarm clock," Dink said.

"It is," Officer Fallon said. "It's an alarm clock with the volume set on loud. I'm guessing the kidnapper tossed it into Ping's cave, knowing the pandas would run out when the thing went off. He probably grabbed Winnie as she came out of the cave."

"And if we want her back," Dink said, "Green Lawn has to pay a million dollars!"

"You're right," Officer Fallon said, "unless we find the bad guy first."

"But we only have till midnight," Ruth Rose said. She looked at her watch. "That's only twelve hours from now!"

THE PANDA PAPER

PETTING ZOO PERFECT PLACE FOR PANDAS!

CHAPTER 3

"I'm hungry," Nate announced. "Can we go home?"

"Okay," said Ruth Rose. "I'll make us some sandwiches."

"And I've got to get to my office and check these things for fingerprints," Officer Fallon said. "But unless this guy was stupid, he'd have worn gloves."

They separated at the police station. Dink, Josh, Ruth Rose, and Nate headed for Woody Street.

At Ruth Rose's house, the kids made lunch. Nate took his sandwich to the living room to watch a dinosaur video.

Dink, Josh, and Ruth Rose ate theirs at the kitchen table. Pal snoozed at Josh's feet.

"It's almost one o'clock," Dink said. "Eleven hours till midnight."

"So where do we start looking for a panda kidnapper?" asked Josh.

"It could be anyone!" Dink said.

Ruth Rose chewed slowly. "Not anyone," she said after a minute. "If that knife really was the kidnapper's, maybe he's a fisherman."

"Or a fisherwoman," said Josh.

Ruth Rose nodded. "Good point."

"Whoever it was either has a key to the gate or can climb over tall fences," Josh went on. He reached for another sandwich. "So who does that narrow it down to?"

"Anyone," Ruth Rose said glumly.

Nate screeched from the living

room. "Dinosaur fight! Come see, you guys!"

Josh ran to the living room, with Dink and Ruth Rose following.

On the TV screen, a Tyrannosaurus and a Stegosaurus were circling each other. Their tails lashed back and forth. The Tyrannosaurus roared and snapped his enormous teeth.

Then the dinosaurs were gone, and the scene switched to a museum. A man's face appeared on the screen. "Hello, I'm Dr. Paleo," he said, "and I'd like to talk to you about what you just saw in this video."

An idea popped into Dink's head. "Ruth Rose, didn't you tape what happened at Panda Park this morning? Why don't we watch your video? Maybe we'll see some clues."

"Good idea," Ruth Rose said. "Do you mind, Natie?"

"Can I have a cookie?" Nate asked, grinning at his sister.

"Sure. Bring the box in here so we can all have some, okay?"

"O-kay!" Nate said, racing toward the kitchen.

Ruth Rose ejected the dinosaur video, then plugged the camcorder into the VCR.

Nate came back with the cookie box. Josh reached for one as Ruth Rose hit the Play button.

The kids watched as Tom Steele, Irene Napper, and Flip Frances came on the screen. Seconds later, Ping emerged from her cave.

Ping looked around, froze, then turned her head sharply. Suddenly she rushed forward and began throwing herself against the fence.

"She sure looks angry," Dink said.

"You'd be mad, too, if someone stole

your baby," Josh said. "It looks like she's trying to attack someone outside the fence."

"Someone in the crowd?" Ruth Rose asked.

"She's not looking at the crowd," Dink said. He put his finger on the TV screen. "Remember, the microphone was there, off to the side. That's where she's looking."

"She's mad at the microphone?" Josh asked, grabbing two more cookies.

"Dink's right!" Ruth Rose said. "Ping is looking at the people standing at the microphone."

Dink, Josh, and Ruth Rose stared at the TV screen.

Finally, Ruth Rose unplugged the camcorder and put Nate's dinosaur tape back into the VCR.

"I think one of those three people kidnapped Winnie," she said, "and Ping knows which one."

CHAPTER 4

"You think Winnie's kidnapper was standing right there at the microphone?" Dink asked.

Ruth Rose nodded. "Yes, and I think Ping recognized him or her. That's why she charged the fence!"

"But the guy probably stole Winnie at night," Dink said, "so how could Ping have seen him?"

"Maybe she didn't see him," Ruth Rose said, "but she might have smelled him."

"Right," Josh said. "Most animals

can smell a lot better than humans."

Dink stared at the TV screen. "So how do we figure out who Ping was growling at?" he asked.

"Too bad pandas can't talk," Josh said. "We could just ask her!"

"Pandas can't talk," Ruth Rose said, "but *people* can. I say we interview the three people who were standing at the microphone, starting with Irene Napper."

"You think she did it?" Dink asked.

"I don't know," Ruth Rose said. "But she *does* have a key to the gate."

"If she thinks we suspect her, she might clam up," Josh said.

Ruth Rose pointed at Dink's notebook. "We'll tell her we're writing a story for *The Panda Paper*."

"Good idea," Dink said.

Josh stood up and patted his stomach. "I have to be home by four to watch the twins for an hour," he said.

Ruth Rose grabbed the cookie box. It was empty! "Joshua, I didn't get a single cookie!" she said.

Josh grinned. "Detective work makes me hungry!"

Josh woke up Pal, and the kids left Ruth Rose's house. They took a shortcut through the rose garden in Center Park. Pal barked at a swan being trailed by three cygnets.

They passed the Book Nook and waved at Mr. Paskey in his window.

At the petting zoo, they passed under a wooden arch. A honeysuckle vine climbed the arch, filling the air with a sweet smell. A hummingbird darted away.

They found Irene Napper surrounded by ducks. She was feeding them pellets that she pulled from one of her uniform pockets.

"Hi, Ms. Napper," Ruth Rose said.

"Well, hi," Irene said. "Say, weren't you kids at Panda Park this morning?"

"Yeah. We're sorry about the kidnapping," Josh said.

Irene's smile disappeared. "I'm so angry I don't know what to do!" she said. "Who would steal a baby panda?"

No one knew what to say. "Good thing Winnie's old enough to eat bamboo," Irene said. "If she still needed her mother's milk, I don't think she'd make it."

Ruth Rose nudged Dink.

"Um, we're writing a story for *The Panda Paper*," Dink said. "Could we ask you some questions?"

The woman looked at Dink for a moment. "Yeah, I guess," she said finally.

Just then, Pal barked, and the ducks scattered.

"But first let's move your dog away from my ducks," Irene said.

The kids followed Irene to a shady bench. She sat and stretched out her long legs.

"Shoot," Irene said.

Pal sighed and dropped to the ground. Irene started stroking his ears. Dink noticed that Irene's hands were large and strong-looking.

Everyone was waiting for Dink to ask a question. But Dink's mind was suddenly blank.

"Who takes care of Ping and Winnie?" Ruth Rose asked, coming to Dink's rescue.

"I do," Irene said. "I feed them, clean out their area, all that stuff. Ping even let me hold her baby."

Dink wrote down what Irene said. Then he asked, "When did you last see Winnie?"

"Last night," Irene said, "when I added fresh water to their pool. That was about eight o'clock."

"So someone snatched her between then and ten o'clock this morning," Ruth Rose said.

Irene nodded. Dink thought she might cry.

Dink had his next question all ready. "How many people have keys to the gate?" he asked.

Irene looked at him. "Only me," she said finally. She patted a key ring hanging from her belt. "And trust me, this was *never* out of my sight. Whoever took Winnie didn't unlock that gate."

A duck waddled over and pecked at Irene's boot. She reached into her pocket, found a few more pellets, and flung them to the ground.

"I've got to get back to work," she said, standing up. She glanced down at Dink's notebook. "Good luck with your story!"

"Thanks," Dink said. "By the way, do you know where Tom Steele lives?"

Irene shook her head. "No, but you'll probably find him in his office."

Dink looked blank. "His office?"

"It's in the senior community center," Irene said. She gave him a suspicious look. "I'm surprised you don't know that, since you're writing a story for him."

CHAPTER 5

Dink had to think fast. "Tom Steele doesn't know we're doing a story," he said. "We just decided to write it a little while ago. We're hoping he'll publish it."

"Does he work on Sundays?" Ruth Rose asked.

"I wouldn't be surprised," Irene said. "Especially after what happened to Winnie."

The kids thanked Irene and headed out of the petting zoo. Pal trotted behind Josh with his long ears nearly touching the ground.

"Think she's the kidnapper?" Dink asked.

"I do!" said Josh. "Did you see the size of her hands? She could kidnap a crocodile!"

"It could be her," Ruth Rose said. "She's the only one with a key."

"I don't know," Dink said. "She really seems to like animals."

"Maybe she likes money better," Josh said, wiggling his eyebrows.

They entered the senior community center through a rear door. Dink spotted a sign saying THE PANDA PAPER and an arrow pointing down a hallway.

"Um, what do we ask this guy?" Josh whispered. Pal sniffed the floors as they walked.

"For one thing," Dink said, "I'll ask him if he'll put my story in his paper."

"The one you haven't written yet?" Josh asked with a grin.

"Yeah, that one," said Dink.

Soft guitar music greeted them at an open door. Tom Steele was sitting at a computer with his back to the kids. A small radio sat on the desk.

Dink knocked on the doorjamb. The editor went on typing. He was humming along with the tune.

"Come on," Ruth Rose said, and she walked into the room.

Tom Steele whirled around in his chair. "You scared me!" he said. He stood up and stared at the kids.

He was probably only a little taller than Dink, but his spiky hair and cowboy boots added another three inches.

He wore round glasses under thick eyebrows that met in the middle. One of his hands had a Band-Aid across the palm.

"Sorry," Dink said. "I'm Dink Duncan and, um, I'm writing a story about Winnie. This morning, you said you wanted stories, so I—"

Tom raised one hairy eyebrow at Dink. "You're a writer?"

"Not yet, but I want to be when I grow up," Dink said.

Tom glanced down at Pal. "Who's this?"

"His name's Pal," Josh said. "He used to belong to crooks!"

"Hmph," Tom said, sitting back down. He removed his glasses, leaned back, and plunked his boots on the top of his desk. The desk was littered with papers, scissors, a bottle of glue, pencils, and an oily pizza box.

Tom held up an issue of *The Panda Paper*. There were holes in the paper where sections had been cut out.

"Have you been reading any of these?" he asked.

"We read them all," Ruth Rose said. She showed Tom her own copy.

"We like pandas," Josh said.

Tom squinted his eyes. He stared at the tips of his boots. The only noise in the room was the ticking of a clock. "I like pandas, too," he said finally. "If I get my hands on whoever kidnapped Winnie . . ."

He rubbed his face. "Okay, write your story. If it's good, I'll print it."

"Could we ask a few questions?" Dink pulled his notebook from a pocket.

Tom sighed and glanced at his watch. "I guess I can spare a few more minutes," he said.

"Do you know anyone who has a

key to the panda enclosure?" Dink asked.

"Yeah, Irene Napper does," he said. "I think she's the only one."

Dink nodded.

"Have you ever noticed anyone weird hanging around Panda Park?" Josh asked.

Tom shook his head slowly. "Just normal-looking people like you and me," he said, grinning.

"Were you surprised when Ping got upset this morning?" Ruth Rose asked.

"Sure, we all were," Tom said. "Flip told me he'd never seen her so angry."

"Does Flip Frances visit the pandas a lot?" Josh asked.

Tom stood up. "I have no idea," he said, "and I have to get back to work." He stuck out his left hand to shake. "Excuse the wrong hand. I got a bad paper cut on the other one."

"Thanks, Mr. Steele," Dink said, shaking the hand. He hesitated, then added, "Do you know where we can find Flip Frances?"

"Flip works at the fitness center," Tom said, pointing toward Main Street.

Ruth Rose took a close look at the top of Tom's desk. "Are you going to write a story about the kidnapping, Mr. Steele?" she asked.

The man nodded toward the mess on his desk. "That's what I'm doing right now," he said. "So if you'll excuse me . . ."

Dink promised to bring his story by in a couple of days, and the kids left. They hurried back down the hall, out the back door, and into the sunshine.

"He's the one," Josh announced. "That Band-Aid gave it away. Paper cut, my aunt Fanny! I bet Winnie bit his hand when he grabbed her."

"He had scissors and glue on his desk, and he was cutting out newspaper clippings," Ruth Rose said. "The ransom note had letters cut out of newspapers!"

"And did you guys see what was leaning in the corner?" Josh asked.

"No, but you're going to tell us, right?" Dink said.

"A fishing pole!" Josh said. "And that was a fishing knife Pal found in the bamboo. I say we call the cops!"

"I don't know," Dink said. "This guy has a hurt hand. And he'd need both hands if he was climbing a fence carrying a panda."

Josh smirked. "Ever heard of ladders?"

Dink grinned at his friend. "What, the guy carries a ladder, an alarm clock, a knife, and a panda? Maybe we should be looking for a juggler!"

THE PANDA PAPER

PETTING ZOO PERFECT PLACE FOR PANDAS!

CHAPTER 6

A sign outside the fitness center said NO
PETS, NO BARE FEET, NO SMOKING.

Josh tied Pal to a tree, patted his
head, and said, "Stay, boy."

Pal sighed and flopped down. His
big brown eyes watched Josh, Dink,
and Ruth Rose enter the building.

The fitness center was one enormous room. One end was filled with
exercise equipment. A bank of windows looked out at Wren Drive.

A shimmery pool took up the other

end of the room. A lifeguard watched three swimmers doing laps.

Other people were using the weights and machines. The clang of metal hitting metal fought with the rock music blaring from hidden speakers.

Dink wrinkled his nose. He smelled a combination of sweat and chlorine.

A green awning was stretched over a counter where juice and health foods were being sold.

"I need a milkshake!" Josh said, shouting above the music. "I feel weak."

"They sell health shakes," Ruth Rose informed him. "They make 'em from seaweed and tofu."

"What's tofu?"

Ruth Rose giggled. "It's white and wiggly," she said. "You'd hate it, Josh."

"There's Flip," Dink said, "behind the counter."

Flip Frances was wearing a T-shirt and blue shorts. He had long, muscular arms. "Can I help you kids?" he asked.

"Hi, Mr. Frances," Dink said. "I'm writing a story about the pandas. Could we interview you?"

"Call me Flip," the man said, smiling at Dink. "Who're you?"

"Call him Dink," Josh said, eyeing the shake machine.

Flip noticed and asked, "You guys thirsty? How about a shake on me?"

"Sure!" Josh said. "But no tofu, please. Or seaweed."

Flip Frances laughed. "How about milk, yogurt, and strawberries?"

"Now you're talking!" Josh said, hoisting himself onto a stool.

Flip expertly tossed ingredients into a blender. He switched it on for a minute, then poured the frothy pink concoction into three tall glasses.

"We were there this morning," Dink said.

Flip slid the shakes and a jar of straws in front of the kids. "My granny Win would be broken-hearted if she knew," he said.

The kids began drinking. Josh made loud slurping noises through his straw.

Dink picked up his pencil. "Why do they call you Flip?" he asked.

"I work out a lot on the floor mats,"

Flip said. He grinned. "I guess I'm famous for my back flips. Why do they call you Dink?"

Josh started to laugh and choked on his shake.

"My real name is Donald David Duncan," Dink told him. "I guess Dink is easier."

Flip looked at Dink's notebook. "So how much have you written?" he asked.

"Not much," Dink said. "We're talking to people who know Winnie."

"Did your grandmother like pandas?" Ruth Rose asked. "Is that why she left all that money?"

Flip nodded. "Granny Win loved animals," he said. "She used to donate money to animal shelters all the time."

Dink glanced at his notes about Irene Napper. "Do you know who has keys to the panda enclosure?" he asked.

Flip nodded. "Yup. Irene has one. I don't know who else."

"Have you seen anybody strange hanging around Panda Park?" Josh asked.

Flip looked up at the ceiling. "Not strange, maybe, but that guy who writes *The Panda Paper* seems to be there a lot. Tom Steele."

In his notebook, Dink wrote TOM STEELE in dark letters.

"Anything else?" Flip asked. "It's almost my lunch break."

The kids finished their shakes. "Thanks a lot," Dink told Flip.

"Glad to do it," he answered.

Just then, a tall redheaded woman approached the counter. She was dressed like Flip, in a T-shirt and blue shorts. "Sorry I'm late," she said to Flip. "You can take off for lunch now."

"No problem, Kate," he said. "Late lunch is better than no lunch."

Flip placed both hands on the

counter and vaulted over. "Good luck with your story," he said to the kids as he strode out the door.

Dink, Josh, and Ruth Rose followed Flip out. They saw him leap into a dusty jeep with a rack on top. He tooted and waved as he pulled onto Bridge Lane.

"Well, what do you think?" Dink asked, watching the jeep turn right on Main Street.

"He gets my vote," Josh said, untying Pal's leash from the tree. "That guy could climb an eight-foot fence with one arm tied behind his back."

Ruth Rose laughed. "Joshua, ten minutes ago you said the kidnapper was Tom Steele."

"Yeah," Dink said, "and before that, you were sure it was Irene Napper!"

"So who do you think it is?" Josh asked.

"It could be any of them," Dink said with a sigh. He shoved his notebook into his back pocket.

"Did you guys notice that rack on Flip's jeep?" Ruth Rose asked. "I wonder if that's for a boat."

"I don't get it," Josh said.

"Maybe Flip is a fisherman, Josh," Ruth Rose said. "Remember the knife?"

"Wait a sec," Dink said. He zipped back inside the fitness center.

Kate looked up and smiled at him. "Come to work out? Kids get in free after three o'clock on Sundays." She slid three passes across the counter.

"Thanks," Dink said, slipping the passes into a pocket. Then he crossed his fingers behind his back. "Flip said something about going fishing later. Do you know if he has a boat?"

"Just an old canoe," she said. "But he can't go fishing. He's working all day."

Dink felt himself blush. "Oh, um, maybe I made a mistake. See ya!" He darted back outside.

"Canoe," he said.

"See!" Josh crowed.

"That doesn't prove anything," Dink said. "All three of the people we talked to could have done it."

"And time is running out for Winnie," Ruth Rose said. "Eight hours till midnight!"

Josh looked at his watch. "Yikes!" he said, starting to run. "I have to be home in five minutes!"

CHAPTER 7

The kids hurried to Josh's house. His parents were waiting.

"We'll be back in about an hour," Josh's mom told him as she climbed into the family car. Josh's dad waved and pulled out of their driveway.

"I wanna ride the pony!" Brian yelled, tugging at Josh's arm.

"No! I wanna catch turtles in the river!" Brian's twin brother, Bradley, bellowed, yanking the other arm.

"You can't do either one without Mom and Dad's permission," Josh said.

"Then we get candy!" Brian said.

"No, we get ice cream!" Bradley argued, bolting for the house.

Josh sighed and followed his brothers. Dink and Ruth Rose laughed, trailing after Josh. Inside, Josh poured five glasses of orange juice.

Brian jumped off his chair and ran from the room. He was back in a flash with a flat cardboard box.

"Let me help!" Bradley said.

"No, it's my puzzle!" Brian yelled. "Josh!"

"You guys do the puzzle together or not at all," Josh said, "and don't get your sticky little fingers all over the pieces."

"What's the puzzle, Bradley?" Ruth Rose asked.

"Gwizzly bears!" Bradley answered, dumping the pieces onto the table. The picture on the box top showed a mama grizzly bear and her cub.

The puzzle pieces were large, just right for four-year-old fingers. Brian and Bradley had done this puzzle before. Their hands flew over the pieces, jamming them into place.

A few minutes later, the puzzle was complete, except for one piece. The baby grizzly bear's face was missing.

"You took it!" Brian yelled at Bradley.

"Did not. You did!" Bradley yelled right back.

"Don't argue, guys," Josh said. He dropped down to the floor and looked under the table. "Not here. Maybe it's in your room."

The twins flew out of the kitchen and thundered toward their bedroom.

Twenty seconds later, they charged back into the kitchen. Bradley held the missing piece in his little hand. He lurched back onto his chair and fitted the piece into place.

"Where'd you find it?" Josh asked.

"Under my bed," Bradley said, grinning.

"I wish finding a missing panda bear was that easy," Dink said.

Ruth Rose sat up. "That's it!" she said. "Maybe we should be looking for Winnie, *not* the guy who took her."

"But where?" Dink asked. "He could've stuck her anywhere."

"If I kidnapped a panda bear," Ruth Rose said, "where would I hide it?"

Josh took a bowl of apples out of the refrigerator and gave one to Brian and one to Bradley. "You can feed the cores to the pony," he told them.

The twins shot out the back door, racing each other to the barn. Pal waddled after them.

Dink, Josh, and Ruth Rose took their apples outside. They sat on the back steps and watched the twins pet Polly through the corral rails.

"Baby panda bears aren't house-broken like regular pets," Josh said, munching his apple. "You couldn't really hide one in your house."

"And I bet Winnie misses her mom," Ruth Rose said. "She'd probably cry a lot. People would hear her."

"Right," said Josh. "So the kidnapper probably hid her where it's already noisy."

Dink watched Polly the pony chomp Brian's apple core. "The kidnapper has to feed Winnie, so he'd keep her nearby."

"I know a place," Ruth Rose said. "It's noisy and smelly, and not far away from the petting zoo."

Josh grinned at Ruth Rose. "I do, too. The fitness center, right?"

Ruth Rose nodded. "If Flip stole Winnie, that would be a perfect place to hide her."

"Should we go back and have a look?" Dink asked.

"But what do we do about Flip?" Josh asked. "If he really is the kidnapper, won't he be suspicious when we show up again?"

Dink reached into his pocket and brought out the passes. "Kids get in free today," he said.

"Excellent!" Ruth Rose said. "We can go over for a swim and a snoop!"

The headline on the newspaper reads:

THE PANDA PAPER

PETTING ZOO PERFECT PLACE FOR PANDAS!

CHAPTER 8

The kids met in front of the fitness center an hour later. They were carrying their bathing suits and towels.

Flip and Kate were behind the counter. The gym was crowded, and the music was still blasting.

"Back again?" Flip asked.

Dink laid the three passes on the counter. "We came for a swim," he said.

"Great idea," said Kate. "Come on, I'll show you where to change."

She led the kids toward the pool.

There were a lot of other kids splashing around. A few grown-ups sat on the side, watching. The lifeguard prowled around the pool, keeping a sharp eye on the swimmers.

Kate stopped in front of a row of four doors. Two of them were labeled MEN and WOMEN. But the two doors in the middle were unmarked.

"Here are the changing rooms," Kate said. "No diving, no running, and listen for Danny's whistle. If he blows it once, everyone freeze. Then he'll blow it again twice. That means kids get out of the pool for fifteen minutes while the adults swim. Have a good time!"

"See you in three minutes," Ruth Rose said, and disappeared into the girls' changing room.

Dink and Josh went into theirs and found themselves alone. Blue metal lockers lined the four walls. At the far end were showers, sinks, toilets, and a floor-to-ceiling mirror. The floor was carpeted, and there were benches to sit on.

Dink walked over to a small closet with STORAGE stenciled on the door. He peeked inside.

"See any pandas?" Josh whispered.

Dink glanced at Josh in the mirror. "No, but I see a skinny redheaded monkey."

"You are so dunked when I get you in the pool," Josh said.

The boys changed, stashed their clothes in two lockers, and headed for the pool.

The lifeguard stopped them. "Hi, guys," he said. "I'm sure Kate explained the rules, right? You've got about ten minutes before adult swim. Have fun!"

"Thanks, we will," Dink said.

Ruth Rose came out wearing a lime

STOR

green bathing suit. The kids jumped
into the water at the shallow end.

"Now what?" Josh asked, glancing
toward Flip behind the counter.

"I wonder what's behind those two
other doors," Dink said.

"One might lead to the bowling
alley," Josh said. "I think it's right below
us."

"Maybe we can check them out
during adult swim," Ruth Rose said.

"When the whistle blows, make sure you climb out on that side."

While they waited, the kids swam and splashed each other. Josh tried standing on his head underwater. He came up coughing.

Suddenly the whistle blew.

Everyone in the pool turned and faced the lifeguard. "Adult swim!" he yelled, and blew the whistle twice more.

There was a wet stampede as the kids clambered out of the water. At the same time, the adults tried to climb into the pool.

Most of the confusion was right in front of the changing rooms. No one noticed as Ruth Rose tried the handles on the unmarked doors. One was locked, but the other one opened.

"Come on!" Ruth Rose whispered as she slipped through. Dink and Josh were right behind her.

When Dink pulled the door closed, it was pitch-black.

"Where the heck are we?" Josh asked, shivering. All three kids were dripping pool water.

Dink put his arms out and touched smooth walls on each side. He inched one bare foot forward and felt the edge of a wooden step.

"I think we might be at the top of a staircase," he whispered.

"Let's try to find a light," Josh said. "I hate the dark."

"Not yet," Ruth Rose said. "Let's feel our way down and see if there's a light at the bottom."

"Watch out for slivers," Dink said.

The kids made their way down the dark stairs. They reached a hard, cold floor and stopped.

"Okay, I'm not going any farther without light!" Josh announced. "I feel like one of those blind fish that live in a cave."

They felt around on the walls.

"Got it," Ruth Rose said. There was a click, and the lights came on.

The kids were standing at one end of a corridor. The floor was smooth stone. The bottom half of the walls was rougher stone, with newer-looking painted boards on the top. The ceiling was a mess of ancient wooden beams, rusty pipes, and spider webs.

"Check this out," Dink said. Scratched into the mortar between two stones was a date: 1902. "This wall was built a hundred years ago!"

"And it's still creepsville," Josh said through chattering teeth. "These stones are c-cold!"

The narrow corridor was filled with broken gym equipment, rolled-up floor mats, and large paint containers. A row of cardboard boxes lined the right-hand wall.

There were no other doors in the corridor.

"What's that noise?" Ruth Rose asked. "It sounds like thunder."

Dink leaned his head against the wall on his left. "I think the bowling alley is on the other side," he said.

The kids began walking along the hallway.

"Let's look in every box," Ruth Rose

said. "Winnie's small, so she could be hidden anywhere."

Five minutes later, they'd run out of boxes. Most had been empty, but a few held white packing peanuts. The kids stood at the end of the corridor and thought about what to do next. A floor mat had been left there. The kids flopped down on it.

Josh rubbed his bare feet and shivered.

"It's weird that they'd have this long hall with no doors," Dink said.

"Maybe it was an old basement before the fitness center got built," Ruth Rose said.

"Ouch!" Josh said.

"Now what?" Dink asked.

"I don't know, but it hurts!" Josh got up and poked the mat where he'd been sitting.

"Help me lift this thing," he said.

"There's something under it."

The kids got up and helped Josh lift the mat. Hidden underneath was the metal handle of a trapdoor.

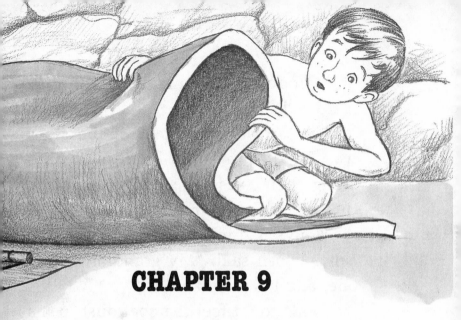

CHAPTER 9

"Should we open it?" Josh asked.

Without answering, Dink grabbed the handle and pulled. The door came up easily. Beneath it were stone stairs leading down. They heard something skittering about in the darkness below.

"Yuck, rats!" Josh said. "If you think I'm going—"

"Shhh, I heard something else!" Ruth Rose said.

Then they all heard it. It was a squeaking, crying noise.

"That's Winnie!" Ruth Rose said.

She ran down the stairs. Dink and Josh were right behind her.

The air at the bottom of the steps was filled with some kind of dust. It stung their eyes. The only light came through the open trapdoor.

"Guys, I think we're in an old coal cellar," Josh said. "My grandfather has one, and it's just like this!"

Dink could feel the coal dust in his eyes and nose and on his lips. He began to cough.

"Look, there's Winnie!" Ruth Rose whispered. Across the room glowed a pair of eyes.

Suddenly the trapdoor slammed shut. Instantly they were in total darkness. Then they heard the sound of metal on metal.

"Someone locked us in!" Josh said. "I can't see anything!"

"Let's not panic, okay?" Ruth Rose said.

"Let's just sit down where we are," Dink suggested.

"But I can't see!" Josh complained. "This place is disgusting!"

Dink sat down. Underneath him, he felt a few lumps of coal. He brushed them aside.

"I'll bet Flip locked us in," Ruth Rose said. "He must have figured out where we went."

Dink heard Josh standing up. "What're you doing, Josh?"

"This building is old, so maybe the lock is, too," Josh said. "I might be able to force it."

"I'll help you," Dink said. He and Josh stumbled up the steps and shoved against the trapdoor. It didn't move.

"Well, it was a good idea, Josh," Dink said.

They found their way back down the steps and sat next to Ruth Rose.

"How are we supposed to get out of

here?" Josh asked in a shaky voice.

"Maybe there's a window," Ruth Rose said. "Don't basements have windows?"

"But it's not a basement," Josh said. "It's just a room where they kept the coal in the old days."

"I bet no one ever comes down here anymore," Dink said. "It was a good place to hide Winnie."

"Where is she, I wonder?" Ruth Rose said.

"She's probably hiding," Dink said. "If only we had a light."

"Gee, if I'd known I was gonna be trapped underground," Josh said, "I'd have brought my flashlight."

"Don't worry," Ruth Rose said. "Flip will let us out after he collects his money at midnight."

"Well, I'm not sitting here till midnight," Josh said, standing up again. "I have a plan!"

"You do?" Dink said.

"Yeah," Josh said, sliding lumps of coal out of the way with his bare feet. "Let's hold hands and try to find the walls. Then we can feel around the whole room."

"What're we feeling for?" Ruth Rose asked.

"The coal chute," Josh said.

"The coal shoot?" Dink said. "Like in a gun?"

"The coal *chute,* Dinkus. C-H-U-T-E," Josh said. "My grandfather told me how coal used to get delivered. They slid it down a chute right into the basement."

"So you're saying there's one of those slide things here somewhere?" Ruth Rose asked.

"Yeah, and it'll lead to the outside!"

The kids held hands, with Ruth Rose in the middle. Dink and Josh reached out and groped for the walls.

Seconds later, Dink tripped over

something. He landed on his knees in a pile of coal.

"I found a shovel," Dink said, running a hand over the metal shape.

He used the shovel to help him stand. He lost his balance and fell against a wall.

"Okay," he said, rubbing his elbow. "I found a wall. Now what?"

"Feel along for some kind of opening," Josh said. "It might be kind of high up."

All three kids moved along the wall, feeling their way. Dink used the shovel like a cane as he shuffled along.

Once Dink heard a whimper. "It's okay, Winnie," he said into the darkness. "We're the good guys."

Suddenly Ruth Rose shouted, "I FOUND SOMETHING!"

"What's it feel like?" Josh asked.

"Like a window frame," she said.

"But there's no glass—there's a piece of board or something where the glass should be."

"That must be the chute," Josh said. "How high up is it?"

"A little above my head," Ruth Rose said. "But I can reach it."

Dink and Josh felt their way along the wall until they were standing next to Ruth Rose.

"I think you found it, Ruth Rose," Josh said. "But how do we get it open?"

Dink lifted the heavy metal shovel. "Will this do?" he asked.

CHAPTER 10

Dink felt the wood that covered the chute. "It feels old," he said. "Back away, you guys. I'll smack it with the shovel."

"How will you hit anything?" Ruth Rose asked. "I can't even see you!"

Dink felt the chute again, judging its distance. He raised the shovel over his head, swung, and missed.

"Pretend you're blindfolded and you're swinging at a pinata," Josh said. "It's filled with candy, money, cookies . . ."

THWACK!

Dink's second swing struck something solid. Now that he had the right location, he was able to hit it every time he swung.

"See if it's loose," Dink said, out of breath.

"Wait a minute," Ruth Rose said. She stepped forward and felt for the wood. "I think you cracked it!"

"Okay, get back again," Dink said. He swung the shovel with all his might. This time, the wood shattered.

"You got it!" Josh said, pulling broken wood away. "Oh, gross, there's something slimy on me!"

As he spoke, a pile of wet stuff fell into the room. It smelled worse than the coal dust. A beam of sunlight fell through the chute. At Josh's feet was a pile of rotted leaves.

"You did it, Dink!" Ruth Rose cried. Then she started to laugh.

"What?" Josh asked.

"Our legs and feet are black! We look like pandas!"

The kids stared up at the sunlight. The chute was slanted. It was easy to see how coal would come sliding down into the cellar.

"We need something to climb on," Josh said.

"All we have is the coal," Ruth Rose said.

"And my handy-dandy coal shovel!" Dink added. "What if we make a pile right under the opening?"

"But how do we climb out?" Ruth Rose asked. "The chute is steep and looks slippery."

"We can boost each other up," Josh said. "The first one out can pull up the next one. The ones on the inside can push."

"But how about the last person?" Ruth Rose asked. "Who boosts him up? And what about Winnie?"

"I guess somebody has to stay here while the others get help," Dink said.

The kids stood and thought, with the sunlight streaming down through the chute.

"How's this?" Josh said after a

minute. "Ruth Rose, you're the smallest. What if Dink and I boost you through the chute? We can stay here with Winnie while you run to the police station."

"Are you sure?" Ruth Rose asked. "Maybe you should go. You're a faster runner."

"Nah, I have to stay to protect Dink," Josh said. "He's afraid of the dark."

"Okay, let's get to work," Dink said. "We'll take turns shoveling."

Ten minutes later, Ruth Rose stood on a small mountain of coal. She stuck her arms into the chute, then her head and shoulders. "Okay, push, you guys!"

Dink and Josh pushed Ruth Rose until only the bottoms of her feet were sticking out of the chute. "More!" she said, her voice sounding hollow. "I can't reach the other end."

As the boys pushed the bottoms of her feet, Ruth Rose inched up the chute. "Okay!" came her faraway voice.

Dink could hear her scrambling to pull herself out. When he and Josh looked up the chute, they saw her face at the other end. "Try to find Winnie," she said. Then she was gone.

Dink and Josh sat on the coal they'd piled up. Neither wanted to leave the comforting shaft of sunlight.

"How do we find a black-and-white panda who's now all black?" Josh asked.

"Maybe if we're real quiet, we'll hear her," Dink said.

They sat totally still on their hill of coal. The sunlight fell between them, bouncing off the shiny black chunks.

Dink heard his own breathing and Josh's. But try as he might, he couldn't hear anything else.

Then Josh giggled.

"What's funny?" Dink asked, glancing over at Josh.

A coal-black baby panda had crawled onto Josh's lap. It was snuggling up against him.

"Winnie must think you're her mama," Dink said. "Boy, do I wish I had Ruth Rose's camcorder now!"

Dink and Josh sat and cuddled with Winnie. The sunlight coming through the chute warmed them up.

Dink heard something over his head. "Listen," he whispered.

"Sounds like someone walking," Josh said, holding Winnie tighter.

Suddenly they heard the trapdoor opening and more light fell into the room.

"Dink? Josh?" It was Ruth Rose's voice. "I brought Officer Fallon!"

THE PANDA PAPER

PETTING ZOO PERFECT PLACE FOR PANDAS!

CHAPTER 11

"If it hadn't been for you kids, Flip would have gotten away with it," Officer Fallon said later that evening.

Dink, Josh, and Ruth Rose were sitting on the lawn at Panda Park. Inside the fence, Ping and Winnie were playing tug-of-war with a stalk of bamboo. Winnie's fur was once again black-and-white.

Dink, Josh, and Ruth Rose were clean, too. A few hours ago, they had surprised their families by showing up completely covered with coal dust.

"He'd have picked up the money at midnight, then let you kids out of the coal cellar," Officer Fallon continued.

"So no one could have proved that he took Winnie or locked us in, right?" Dink asked.

Officer Fallon nodded. "That's right," he said. "No one saw him take Winnie or lock that trapdoor. He'd have hidden the money somewhere. In a year or so, he might have begun spending it."

"Were you really going to leave a million bucks in that hollow tree?" asked Josh.

Officer Fallon nodded. "Flip knew we had no choice," he said.

Just then, Ping yawned, rolled over on her back, and went to sleep. Winnie cuddled next to her and chewed the bamboo stalk.

"Too bad Win Frances isn't here to see this," Dink said.

"Did she leave Flip any money?" Ruth Rose asked.

"Some," Officer Fallon said. "But I guess Flip thought he was entitled to all of it."

"Did he confess?" Josh asked.

Officer Fallon nodded. "You should have seen his face when I walked into that gym with Ruth Rose."

"He thought I was still in the coal cellar," Ruth Rose said. "I must have looked like a ghost!"

"What will happen to him?" Dink asked.

"He'll probably go to jail for attempting to extort money," Officer Fallon said. "Plus, he stole Winnie and trapped you kids in the coal cellar."

Everyone was quiet for a moment.

"Sometimes a judge will give a young person a second chance," Officer Fallon went on, "especially if it's his first crime. Flip seems very sorry for what he did. The judge might ask him to do community service in place of some of his jail time."

"What's community service?" Dink asked.

"That means that Flip would do work for Green Lawn as part of his sentence."

"What kind of work?" Josh asked.

Officer Fallon smiled. "Got any good ideas?"

"I do," Dink said. "He could give free gymnastics lessons to kids."

"And he could help out in the senior center," Josh said. "He could do exercises with the old people."

"I'm sure Flip would be willing. He'd be good at it, too," Officer Fallon said.

"And his grandmother would be proud of him, right?" Ruth Rose asked.

"I knew Win Frances for many years," Officer Fallon said. "She'd be sad about what Flip tried to do. But she was a woman who always gave people the benefit of the doubt. Win would give her grandson a second chance, too."

"So is this what they mean by a

Win-Win situation?" Josh asked.

"Exactly," Officer Fallon said. "Now how about I treat us to ice cream cones at Ellie's?"

"That's a Josh-Josh situation," Dink said, smiling at his friends.

A to Z Mysteries

Dear Readers,

Nicholas Oliverio

So many of you sent in excellent stories for our Alphabet Zweepstakes contest. It was a difficult choice, but I selected Nicholas Oliverio as the winner. His picture is on this page. He sent in a terrific mystery story about a falcon. His winning entry is posted on the Random House Web site at www.randomhouse.com/kids/books/series/az. I loved the story, and I am looking forward to meeting Nicholas and his family when we have lunch in New York City.

This book was about one of my favorite animals, the panda. In doing my research, I discovered that pandas are becoming more and more rare as more and more of their habitat is used for other purposes. I am a member of the World Wildlife Fund, which helps save pandas and other animals from extinction. I have supplied the address below in case you'd like to join, too.

I'm thrilled that so many of you are visiting my Web site and sending me e-mail! I try to answer each one as soon as possible.

That's all for now—I have to get back to work on the next A to Z Mystery.

Happy reading!

Sincerely,

Ron Roy

World Wildlife Fund
1250 24th Street, N.W.
Washington, DC 20037

www.worldwildlife.org

Collect clues with Dink, Josh, and Ruth Rose in their next exciting adventure,

THE QUICKSAND QUESTION

"Wait for me!" Ruth Rose said, kicking off her sandals.

They pushed their feet through the warm, shallow water. Dink could feel the fine sand between his toes. The water was so clear he could see the tiny pebbles on the bottom.

Suddenly Josh stopped. He turned around with panic on his face. "I'm stuck!" he cried.

As Dink watched, Josh started to sink. The water was up to his knees!

"I can't pull my feet out!" Josh yelled. "I think it's quicksand!"

A STEPPING STONE BOOK™

**Great stories by great authors . . .
for fantastic first reading experiences!**

Grades 1–3

FICTION
Nuz Shedd series
  by Marjorie Weinman Sharmat
Junie B. Jones series by Barbara Park
Magic Tree House® series
  by Mary Pope Osborne
Marvin Redpost series by Louis Sachar
Mole and Shrew books
  by Jackie French Koller
Scooter Tales books by Jerry Spinelli

The Chalk Box Kid
  by Clyde Robert Bulla
The Paint Brush Kid
  by Clyde Robert Bulla
White Bird by Clyde Robert Bulla

NONFICTION
Magic Tree House® Research Guides
  by Will Osborne and
  Mary Pope Osborne

Grades 2–4

A to Z Mysteries® series by Ron Roy
Aliens for . . . books
  by Stephanie Spinner & Jonathan Etra
Julian books by Ann Cameron
The Katie Lynn Cookie Company series
  by G. E. Stanley
The Case of the Elevator Duck
  by Polly Berrien Berends
Hannah by Gloria Whelan
Little Swan by Adèle Geras
The Minstrel in the Tower
  by Gloria Skurzynski

Next Spring an Oriole
  by Gloria Whelan
Night of the Full Moon
  by Gloria Whelan
Silver by Gloria Whelan
Smasher by Dick King-Smith

CLASSICS
Dr. Jekyll and Mr. Hyde
  retold by Stephanie Spinner
Dracula retold by Stephanie Spinner
Frankenstein retold by Larry Weinberg

Grades 3–5

FICTION
The Magic Elements Quartet
  by Mallory Loehr
Spider Kane Mysteries
  by Mary Pope Osborne

NONFICTION
Balto and the Great Race
  by Elizabeth Cody Kimmel
The Titanic Sinks!
  by Thomas Conklin

**At first Toots thought it was
a trick of the light.**

She screwed up her eyes, then opened them wide, but it was still there. High in the corner of the ceiling a tiny door had opened, and a creature, no more than half an inch high, had climbed through. Toots could see it as clearly as she could see the books on the bookshelves. The creature was crossing the ceiling and making its way toward the brass lamp in the center, leaving a trail of dark, smudgy footprints on the clean white paint as it did so.

**Discover a hidden world
above and beyond
the ceiling of
your living room in
*Toots and the
Upside-Down House*
by Carol Hughes.**